Published by To God Be The Glory Graphics, LLC
P.O. Box 1479 Ellicott City, MD 21041.

Graphic Editing by Wes Dezyns®.

ISBN 978-0-9992779-5-9

Printed in the U.S.A

Let's Go To D.C.!

By Pat. & Len Moore

Illustrated by Pat. Moore

When our daughter Kimberly was young, she loved to visit Washington, D.C. Her favorite things to do were visit the pandas at the National Zoo, watch fireworks on the 4th of July, explore all the museums on the National Mall, and roll Easter eggs across the White House lawn. It was to those wonderful experiences that we created this book.

Enjoy!

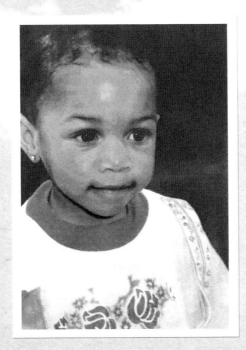

To Tiffany,
Christopher,
Jonathan,
and Kimberly

When it's winter,

Mom says,
"Let's go to D.C.

to see

the
National
Christmas Tree

or take a walk through

DLIGHTS

the
National
Zoo."

When it's spring,

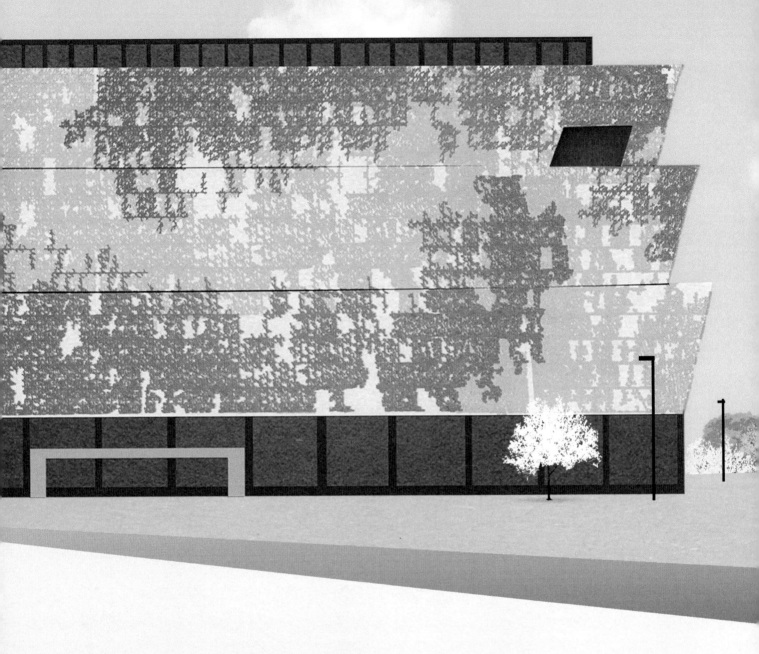

Dad says,
"Let's go to D.C.

to fly our kites

way up high

or see a
cherry blossom

or two."

When it's summer,

Mom says,
"Let's go to D.C.

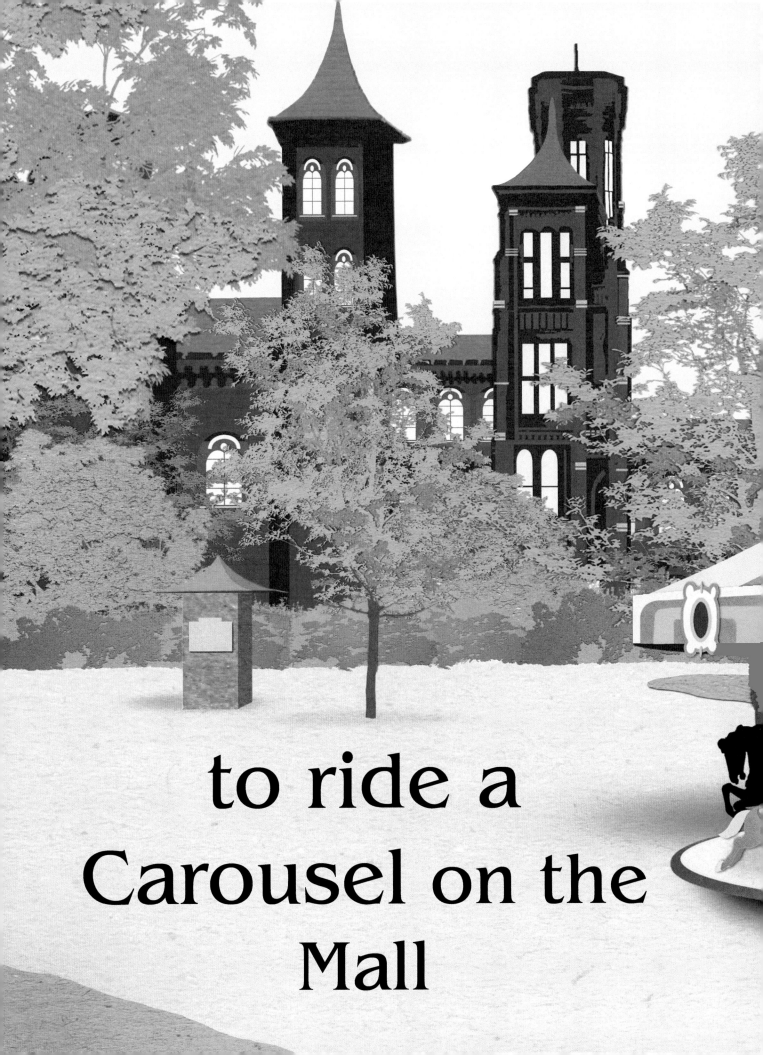

to ride a Carousel on the Mall

or count fireworks

in the sky!"

When it's fall,

We all say,
"Let's go to D.C.

NATIONAL
BOOK FESTIVAL

to read a book

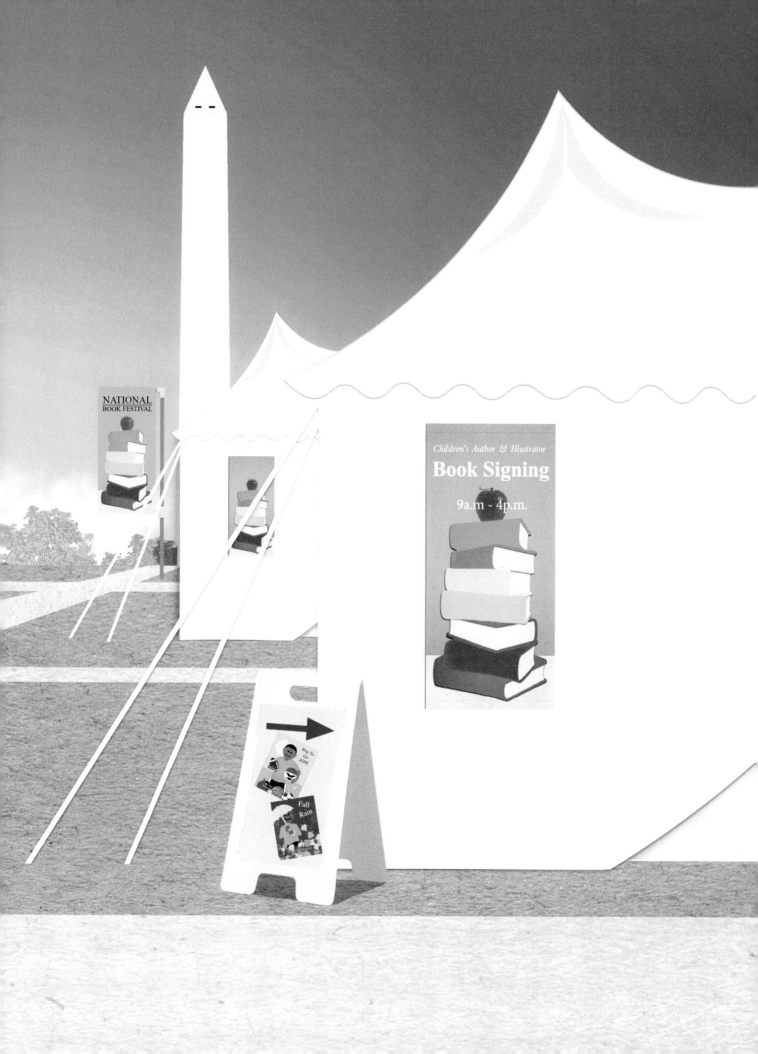

or watch the ducks

go by."

Trust in the Lord with all your heart, and lean not on your own understanding; In all your ways acknowledge Him, and He shall direct your paths.

Proverbs 3:5-6

Made in the USA
Columbia, SC
15 November 2020